Baseball Blues

The Bobbseys and Kevin Frazier were seated at a picnic table. Suddenly Chief, the twins' sheepdog puppy, went running past them. In his mouth was a white ball.

"I hope that's not your autographed baseball, Kevin," Nan said. She jumped up.

All four Bobbseys took off after their pet. After a long chase, they managed to corner Chief and take the ball out of his mouth. "It's just an ordinary baseball," Freddie said.

Halfway back to the tables, the twins ran into Kevin. "Did you find it?" he asked anxiously.

"Isn't your ball back in the tent, where you left it?" Nan asked, frowning.

Kevin shook his head. "No," he said. "My Johnny Kellogg baseball is gone!"

Books in The New Bobbsey Twins™ Series

#1   The Secret of Jungle Park
#2   The Case of the Runaway Money
#3   The Clue That Flew Away
#4   The Secret in the Sand Castle
#5   The Case of the Close Encounter
#6   Mystery on the Mississippi
#7   Trouble in Toyland
#8   The Secret of the Stolen Puppies
#9   The Clue in the Classroom
#10 The Chocolate-covered Clue
#11 The Case of the Crooked Contest
#12 The Secret of the Sunken Treasure
#13 The Case of the Crying Clown
#14 The Mystery of the Missing Mummy
#15 The Secret of the Stolen Clue
#16 The Case of the Disappearing Dinosaur
#17 The Case at Creepy Castle
#18 The Secret at Sleepaway Camp
#19 The Show-and-Tell Mystery
#20 The Weird Science Mystery
#21 The Great Skate Mystery
#22 The Super-duper Cookie Caper
#23 The Monster Mouse Mystery
#24 The Case of the Goofy Game Show
#25 The Case of the Crazy Collections

Available from MINSTREL Books

THE NEW

BOBBSEY

T?W•I•N•S™

#25

The Case of the Crazy Collections

LAURA LEE HOPE

Illustrated by DAVID F. HENDERSON

A MINSTREL® BOOK

PUBLISHED BY POCKET BOOKS

New York   London   Toronto   Sydney   Tokyo   Singapore

A MINSTREL PAPERBACK *ORIGINAL*

 A Minstrel Book published by
POCKET BOOKS, a division of Simon & Schuster Inc.
1230 Avenue of the Americas, New York, NY 10020

ISBN: 0-671-73037-1

First Minstrel Books printing August 1991

10 9 8 7 6 5 4 3 2 1

Contents

1. Collection Time 1

2. Foul Play 11

3. Who's Got the Ball? 19

4. Lightning Strikes Twice 29

5. Sneaking Suspicions 38

6. Buried Treasure 46

7. Looking for Trouble 55

8. If the Shoe Fits 64

9. Caught! 73

10. The Game Is Up 81

**The
Case of the
Crazy
Collections**

1

Collection Time

"Hey, Flossie! Come here and help me!" Freddie Bobbsey called from the front steps of his house. He was trying to carry a bunch of boxes and keep them from falling.

"Sorry," Freddie's twin sister answered. She ran past him, waving a big spoon. "I have to give this to Dad," she called back over her shoulder.

Her blond hair flying, Flossie darted out into the street. This was the day of their neighborhood's yearly block party, so she didn't have to watch for cars. The street was closed off so that all of the neighbors could get together for a few hours.

Freddie glared at Flossie's back and got a grip on the boxes. Then Chief, the Bobbseys' sheepdog puppy, burst out of the house. "Flossie, you forgot to shut the door!" Freddie yelled.

But it was too late. The big puppy knocked Freddie over. All of the boxes went sailing out of his arms. "Oh, no," Freddie groaned.

"Need a hand, Freddie?"

Freddie looked up. One of his neighbors, Mr. Anderson, was hurrying toward him. Mr. Anderson lived in the house at the corner. With him was a short man Freddie didn't know.

"I'll carry a couple of those boxes," Mr. Anderson said. He helped Freddie pick them up.

"Thanks," Freddie said. "They're for my mom. She's in charge of the hot dogs." He pointed to a table in the middle of the block.

Mrs. Bobbsey looked relieved when Freddie and the two men came up to the table. "The rolls are here," she said, taking the boxes. "Thanks."

"Mary, this is an old college friend of mine, Sterling Sher," Mr. Anderson said. "He's staying with us this week."

"It's nice to meet you, Mr. Sher," Mrs. Bobbsey said, shaking his hand.

"Most folks call me Shorty," he said. "I can't imagine why."

The grown-ups laughed. Mr. Sher was shorter than Freddie's mother.

"Hi, everyone." Mr. Bobbsey came over to the table. He was carrying a big pitcher of lemonade.

Behind him, Flossie carried a stack of cups. She and Freddie were going to serve lemonade at the party.

"Excuse me, but I'd better go check the tent," Mrs. Bobbsey said. "I want to make sure it arrived in good condition. The MacKays set it up in their yard this morning."

"I guess we didn't need to rent a tent after all," Mr. Bobbsey said, looking up at the blue sky.

"Amazing—after all that rain yesterday," Mr. Anderson said.

"Lemonade!" Bert Bobbsey jogged up to the table. "I sure am thirsty!" He grinned at Freddie and poured himself a cup.

Nan, his twin, was right behind him. "Me, too!" she said. Nan and Bert were twelve years old. They had dark hair and brown eyes.

"You should see the tent," Nan told Freddie and Flossie. "A bunch of kids are displaying their collections in it. Baseball cards, coins, all sorts of stuff."

"That sounds interesting," Mr. Anderson said. "Want to take a look, Shorty?"

Mr. Sher nodded, and the two men walked off toward the tent.

"They're charging a quarter to get in," Nan said. "The money's going toward a pizza party."

"Why don't you two check it out?" Bert said to the younger twins. "Nan and I will take over for you for a while."

"Thanks!" Flossie said. She and Freddie hurried to the blue- and yellow-striped tent.

Kevin Frazier was seated at a table by the front of the tent. He was a fourth grader at Freddie and Flossie's school. "Hi, guys," he said. He held out his hand. "Admission is twenty-five cents."

4

Flossie reached into her pocket and pulled out two quarters.

"Thanks," said Kevin, taking the money. "We'll count you in for the pizza party."

"Where'd you get all this stuff?" Freddie asked. He was pointing to some old comics and baseball cards.

"From my grandfather," Kevin said. "I even have a baseball signed by Johnny Kellogg."

Freddie let out a whistle. "Cool," he said, picking up the ball to look at the signature.

"Hi, Elizabeth," Flossie called to Elizabeth Chin. She was at the next table. "Those are cute dolls!"

Elizabeth had lots of dolls dressed in fancy costumes. "Thanks," Elizabeth said. "They're all from different countries."

"Hey, Freddie!" a boy called.

Freddie turned and saw six-and-a-half-year-old Marty Peck standing behind a table filled with junk. At least, it looked like junk to Freddie—lots of soda cans and gum wrappers.

"Hi, Marty," Freddie said, walking over to him. "Is this your collection?"

"Part of it," Marty said with a shrug. "My mom wouldn't let me bring my erasers or my rubber bands or my paper clips. I brought my best hologram sticker, though. See?" He handed Freddie a sticker with a huge dinosaur on it.

"Check this out, too," he added. "It's a gum wrapper from Greece." He showed Freddie a paper with strange writing on it.

"Neat," Freddie said.

Flossie came up as he was leaving Marty's table. "Jennifer Silverstein has some real cool autographs," she said. "But she won't let anybody touch them." Flossie made a face. Jennifer was not Flossie's favorite person.

Freddie headed over to Jennifer's table to look at the autographs. "My uncle works in Hollywood, so I have lots of famous people," Jennifer said.

Freddie admired the autographs. Then he moved on to Darryl Williams's table.

Flossie followed him. "Jennifer Silverstein is so snobby," she said in a low voice.

Freddie shrugged. He was more interested in looking at Darryl's collections. Darryl had some old-fashioned piggy banks and a bunch of old coins. "These coins are worth a bundle," Darryl told him.

Carol Meeker's table was next. Dozens of tiny objects, from a miniature piano to itty-bitty groceries, were laid out on a tray.

But as Freddie picked up a mini freight train, he heard angry voices. He turned around quickly. Danny Rugg and Kevin's cousin Steve Frazier were standing by the entrance. They were arguing with Kevin. Freddie frowned when he saw Danny. Danny was the biggest bully in Lakeport.

"You already owe me three dollars, Steve," Kevin was saying. "I'm not loaning you any more money."

"Why do we have to pay, anyway?" Danny grumbled. "We brought a collection just like everybody else."

"Look, Danny," Kevin said. "Four Popsicle sticks is *not* a collection. Besides, those are from this morning. I saw you guys eating them."

Freddie walked up to the bigger boys. "You don't even live on this block, Danny," he said.

"So what, pipsqueak?" Danny shot back. "Steve invited me to your dumb party."

"You can be here, Danny," Kevin said. "But you have to pay to see the collections."

Just then Mr. Sher tapped Kevin on the shoulder. "Excuse me, sonny. Is that your Johnny Kellogg baseball?"

"Yes," Kevin answered.

"I'll give you ten dollars for it," Mr. Sher told him.

Freddie's eyes grew wide. Ten dollars was a lot of money.

"Thanks, but I don't want to sell it," Kevin answered. "My grandfather gave it to me."

"Yeah," Steve added. "All *I* got from Gramps was a stupid savings bond."

"How about twenty dollars?" Mr. Sher said.

Again Kevin said no. Freddie couldn't believe it.

"Okay, I'll give you fifty bucks—but that's my last offer," Mr. Sher said.

Kevin shook his head. "Sorry, mister. The baseball's not for sale."

Mr. Sher gave Kevin an angry look. "Young

man," he said, "somebody ought to teach you the value of a dollar." Then he left the tent.

Steve turned to his cousin. "You jerk, Kevin," he said. "You turn down fifty big ones, and you won't even loan me fifty cents."

"Sorry," Kevin told him.

"You little creep," Danny snarled.

Steve scowled at Kevin. "You'd better watch out for your precious baseball, Kevin," he said. "Something just might happen to it!"

2

Foul Play

Freddie watched as Danny and Steve pushed their way back out of the tent.

"Wow!" Flossie said, walking up to Freddie and Kevin. "They look pretty mad."

Marty Peck came over, too. "Boy, Kevin," he said. "I'd keep an eye on that baseball if I were you."

But Kevin didn't look worried. He tossed the ball into the air and caught it. "Oh, don't worry about Steve," he said. "He'd never really do anything. He's just jealous, that's all."

Flossie held out her hand for the ball, and

Kevin handed it to her. "Who's Johnny Kellogg, anyway?" she asked. "I've never even heard of him."

Freddie rolled his eyes. "Don't you know anything about baseball history?" he said. "Johnny Kellogg was one of the greatest hitters who ever played the game."

"He's in the Hall of Fame," Kevin added.

"Oh," Flossie said, handing the ball back. "Is that good?"

Kevin snorted. "As good as you can get," he said. Carefully he placed the ball back on the table.

"So Steve is jealous, huh?" Freddie asked.

Kevin nodded. "Our grandfather gave us a choice. We could have either some of his collectible stuff or a savings bond. Steve took the bond. Then he bugged his parents until they let him cash it in. He spent all the money on video games, and now he's broke."

"He's probably sorry that he didn't take the collectible stuff," Flossie said.

Kevin nodded. "But I know my cousin," he

said. "Steve wouldn't steal or wreck anything. He's not a bad guy, really."

"I'd be careful, anyway," Freddie warned. "Steve might be okay, but you can't trust Danny Rugg for a second."

Now Kevin looked nervous. "I guess you're right."

"Don't worry," Freddie told him. "Flossie and I will keep an eye on Danny for you."

"Really?" Kevin said hopefully.

"Sure," Flossie said. "We'll go spy on him right now!"

Freddie and Flossie ran out of the tent. They found Danny and Steve playing baseball with some of the older boys. Luckily, neither of them went anywhere near the collections tent.

After a while the food bell rang. All the dishes the Bobbseys' neighbors had brought were lined up on long tables at one end of the street.

Freddie and Flossie hurried to take their place in line. "I'm starved," Freddie told Flossie.

"Me, too," Flossie agreed.

"Hey, you guys!" Bert called from behind them. "Where were you?"

"You were supposed to come right back and take over for us!" Nan said. She was standing beside Bert. They both looked mad.

"I went down to the tent, and you weren't even there," Nan added.

"Oops. Sorry," Freddie said, biting his lip. "We forgot."

"But there's a good reason for that," Flossie said quickly. "We're on a case."

"A case?" Bert said, raising his eyebrows. "What case?"

"We'll tell you after we get our food," Freddie said.

The Bobbseys got paper plates and napkins. They filled their plates with hot dogs, cole slaw, and potato chips.

"Let's sit over there," Nan said. She pointed to a group of tables near the front of the tent.

"It's a case, all right," Freddie told the older twins as soon as they sat down. "Mr. Sher—he's a friend of Mr. Anderson's—offered Kevin fifty dollars for that autographed baseball."

"And Steve and Danny were real mad at Kevin," Flossie added. "Steve told Kevin he'd better watch out, or something might happen to his baseball!"

Nan and Bert looked at each other. Then they shook their heads.

"Sorry," Bert said. "It doesn't seem like much of a case to me."

"I think you two just wanted to play detective so we would do your work," Nan said with a grin.

"That's right," Bert said. "In this case, there is no case!"

Nan giggled.

"Maybe you're right," Freddie said with a sigh. "Nothing really did go wrong."

"Well, we *thought* something might," Flossie argued.

"Hi, guys," Kevin Frazier said. He came up to their table with a full plate in his hands. "Is there any room for me?"

"Sure," Freddie said, moving over on the bench. "Is your ball okay?"

"Yup," Kevin said, smiling. "Thanks for keeping an eye on Danny and Steve."

"Freddie told us somebody offered you fifty

dollars for that Johnny Kellogg ball," Bert said. "Is the ball really worth big bucks?"

Kevin shrugged. "I don't know," he said. "But I'm never going to sell it. My grandfather gave it to me."

Suddenly Chief went running past the table with a white ball in his mouth. The Bobbseys rose to their feet. "He's off his leash again!" Bert shouted.

"That's not his ball, either," Flossie said.

"I hope it's not yours, Kevin," Nan said.

Kevin stood up, too. "I'd better go back to the tent to make sure."

"Chief, come back here!" Flossie yelled.

All four Bobbseys took off after their big puppy. After a long chase through backyards and bushes, Bert managed to corner him.

Nan took the ball out of Chief's mouth. "Thank goodness!" she said, still out of breath. "It's just an ordinary baseball."

"Whew," Freddie said, relieved. "Let's go tell Kevin."

Halfway back to the tables, they ran into

Kevin. "Did you find the ball?" he asked anxiously.

"Yes, but don't worry," Flossie said. "It wasn't yours."

Kevin froze. "What do you mean?"

"Isn't your ball back in the tent where you left it?" Nan asked, frowning.

Kevin shook his head. "No," he said. "My Johnny Kellogg baseball is gone!"

3

Who's Got the Ball?

Soon everyone at the party had heard about Kevin's missing baseball. All the kids and even most of the grown-ups stopped eating to look for it. They searched everywhere, but nobody found it.

"I can't believe someone stole that ball," Mrs. MacKay said sadly to her husband. "I mean, everyone here is a neighbor or a friend."

"It sure takes the fun out of a block party," said Mr. Chin.

The whole mood of the party had changed. People weren't talking and laughing anymore. They were standing around, looking sad.

Freddie stared at his plate of food. Even though he'd been hungry when he'd gotten it, he didn't feel like eating anything now.

"Let's not give up," Bert told his sisters and brother. "Maybe we can get the ball back for Kevin. We can check for clues."

"Good idea," said Nan. The younger twins nodded.

"Kids," said Mrs. Bobbsey, who had been talking to some grown-ups. "We've decided to end the party now. It's getting late, anyhow. Would you help us carry our stuff back to the house?"

"In a minute, Mom," Nan said. "We want to search for clues first."

"Okay," Mrs. Bobbsey said. "But when you finish, bring in everything from our table."

"We will," said Flossie.

The twins headed off toward the tent. The kids had almost finished packing up their collections. Now Mr. Bobbsey, Mr. Anderson, and a few of the other neighbors were starting to take the tent down.

"A clue!" Flossie cried. "I see a clue!"

"Where?" Bert asked quickly.

"There! Footprints!" Flossie pointed to a group of footprints near where the entrance to the tent had been. Because it had rained the day before, there were a lot of prints in the dirt.

Nan bit her lip. "Gee, Flossie," she said. "Those are footprints, all right. But remember, everybody who went into the tent had to come this way."

While Nan and Flossie looked near the entrance, Freddie and Bert walked around where the edges of the tent had been.

"Look!" Freddie said suddenly. He reached down and picked a shiny object out of the mud. It was a small, red and black metal pin. On the pin were funny designs, almost like letters.

"This looks like the writing on Marty Peck's gum wrapper," Freddie said.

"Those are Greek letters," Nan told him. "I've seen them on Mr. Stavrakis's newspaper." Mr. Stavrakis worked in the school cafeteria.

Bert turned the pin over. There was no writing on the back of it. "Maybe this came from one of the collections."

"Nobody had any pins, Bert," Nan said. She held out her hand for the pin.

"You're right," Bert admitted. "Oh, well. Nice try, Freddie."

"Let me see," Flossie said.

Nan handed Flossie the pin. "This may not be a clue, but I think we should hold on to it, anyway," Nan said. "You never know. Maybe someone lost it."

"Look, there's Kevin," Flossie said. Kevin was sitting under a tree in the MacKays' backyard. He looked sad.

"Poor Kevin," Nan said.

"Let's see if we can find out anything from him," Bert suggested. "Maybe he knows something we don't know. Hi, Kevin," Bert said as they walked over to him.

"Hi," Kevin mumbled. "I told my grandfather I'd take good care of that ball," he added miserably.

Bert leaned over to talk to him. "Kevin, let's go over this one more time. When did you last see the ball?"

"I told you," Kevin said. "I left it on my table in the tent."

"Who else was there?" Nan asked.

"Just the other collectors," Kevin said. "That's why I thought it was okay to leave it. I thought my stuff would be safe with the other kids."

"When you left, who was there?" Bert asked.

"Jennifer Silverstein, Carol Meeker . . . Marty Peck, too," Kevin told him.

"Any one of them could have taken the ball before leaving to go eat dinner," Nan pointed out.

"Oh, great. This is just great," Kevin said, moaning miserably.

"Freddie and Flossie," Bert said. "You said you were keeping an eye on Steve and Danny.

Where were they after everybody got their food?"

Freddie and Flossie looked at each other. "We were watching them," Flossie said. "But when the food bell rang, we forgot all about Danny and Steve."

Freddie looked at the ground. "Sorry."

"We got hungry," Flossie said. "But we were all sitting right in front of the tent entrance while we ate. How could someone have gotten in without our seeing him?"

"Too bad everyone's gone home," Freddie said, looking down the block. Hardly anyone was left at the party. "Now we can't even talk to the other kids."

"Yeah, I'd like to ask Steve and Danny a few questions right away," Bert said.

"Oh, man, how am I ever going to tell Gramps I don't have the ball anymore?" Kevin said.

"Don't worry, Kevin," Nan said. "We're going to solve this case."

"I bet Steve and Danny got into the tent when no one was looking," Bert said.

Nan sighed. "Well, we'll just have to put them at the top of our list of suspects."

"Hey! Wait a minute! What about Jennifer Silverstein? She collects autographs," Flossie pointed out. "Maybe she wanted the Johnny Kellogg baseball for her collection."

"Good thinking, Flossie," Freddie said. "An autograph is still an autograph, whether it's on paper or on a baseball."

"Hmm," Nan murmured. "Maybe we should split up and each tackle a suspect."

"Good idea, Nan," Bert said. "Steve's in your history class, right? Why don't you keep an eye on him?"

"Ugh," said Nan, making a face. "Do I have to? He's such a jerk."

"I'll tail Danny Rugg—he's even worse," Bert said. "Okay?"

"Deal." Nan nodded. "Freddie and Flossie, you question the other collectors."

Freddie looked at Flossie. He could tell she was thinking the same thing he was. They were

going to start with suspect number one—
Jennifer Silverstein.

After school the next day, Freddie and Flossie
waited near the entrance. "Has she come out
yet?" Flossie asked.

"Not yet," Freddie replied. But just as he
spoke, out came Jennifer. She looked very happy. *Much* happier than usual, in fact.

The twins stood quietly so Jennifer wouldn't
notice them. "Let's go!" Freddie whispered
to Flossie. The two of them took off after
Jennifer.

It was a beautiful afternoon. Jennifer was
swinging her knapsack back and forth, and
humming as she walked.

"What do you think she's so happy about?"
Flossie asked.

"Maybe her new Johnny Kellogg baseball,"
Freddie replied, frowning.

Jennifer turned a corner onto a main street.
By the time the Bobbseys caught up, she was
nowhere in sight. For a minute they thought

they had lost her. Then they saw Jennifer talking to a man inside one of the stores.

"Look!" said Freddie, pointing to the sign in the store window.

It read: Lakeport Hobby Shop—Stamps, Coins, Baseball Items.

4

Lightning Strikes Twice

"Wow!" Freddie said. "I'll bet Jennifer is selling Kevin's baseball right now. Let's go in and stop her!"

Freddie headed for the door, but Flossie grabbed his arm. "Hold on," she said. "What are you going to do in there? Arrest her?"

"Catch her in the act," Freddie answered, looking through the window. "Let's go in."

"But, Freddie," Flossie argued. "The hobby shop is a small store. If Jennifer sees us in there, she'll hide the baseball. She'll pretend she's just looking at stuff."

"She walked up to the man," Freddie said. "Come on, Flossie. I want to know what they're talking about. Maybe she's asking how much money she can get for the ball."

"No, Freddie! If we go in now, she'll know we suspect her. Then we'll never catch her."

Freddie thought it over. He had to admit Flossie was right. It was better to wait.

So they waited. Soon Jennifer came out, wearing a giant smile. When she turned the corner, the twins rushed into the store. Old magazine covers and movie posters covered one wall of the shop. On the other side, all the way to the ceiling, were shelves holding old toys, records, pins, and stamps.

Flossie and Freddie hurried up to the man who worked there. He was standing behind a wooden counter.

"Excuse me," Flossie said in her most polite voice. "Did the girl who was just in here happen to have a baseball with her?"

The man looked down at Flossie over the top of his glasses. "Why do you want to know?" he asked.

Flossie looked confused. "Well, um . . ." she mumbled.

Freddie took over. "Did she ask you about baseballs?" he asked.

The man leaned over the counter. "Young man and young lady," he said. "We don't give out any information about our customers' collections. Many collectors like to keep that information private. Frankly, I don't blame them. Not everybody in this world is honest, you know."

The way he was staring at them made Freddie feel as if *they* were suspects.

"Oh, forget it," Freddie said with a sigh. "Come on, Flossie. We're not getting anywhere here."

"Wait a minute," Flossie said, reaching into her pocket. She held out the pin they'd found outside the tent. "Do you know what this is?" she asked the man.

The man took the pin from Flossie and smiled. "Now, there I can help you. This is a college pin. It's worn by the members of a fraternity, which is a kind of club. The Greek letters tell the name of the fraternity. These pins

aren't worth much, though, if that's why you're asking."

Flossie sighed. "Thanks, anyway," she said. "Come on, Freddie."

When they were back out on the street, Flossie turned to Freddie. "Now what do we do? We know Jennifer stole Kevin's ball, but how can we prove it?"

Freddie frowned. "We don't know for sure if Jennifer did it, Flossie. We're just guessing. I hope Nan and Bert are having better luck."

"Me, too," Flossie said. "So who's next on our list of suspects?"

Freddie reached into his pocket and pulled out the list he had made the night before. "Darryl Williams," he said. "Let's go."

"Hey, kids, how's it going?" he heard someone say. It was Mr. Sher. He winked at Freddie and Flossie as he passed.

"Hi," Flossie said. "We're looking for Kevin Frazier's missing baseball."

Mr. Sher stopped walking. "Oh, I see," he said. He sounded interested. "That was a shame, wasn't it?"

"It sure was," Freddie agreed. "Poor Kevin is really upset about it."

"His grandfather gave him that ball," Flossie added.

Mr. Sher shook his head. "My, my, my. Any luck finding it?"

"Not yet," Freddie admitted.

"Well," said Mr. Sher, "if I see it, I'll be sure to let you know." He walked off, waving back at them as he went.

"Let's go, Flossie," Freddie said.

When the twins reached Darryl's house, the first person they saw was Jennifer Silverstein. She was walking out the front door.

"Wow!" Flossie whispered to Freddie. "Do you see what I see?"

Freddie nodded, his eyes wide with surprise.

"See you, Jenny," Darryl called out.

"Bye!" Jennifer waved, looking back at him as she walked away down the street. She was staring at Darryl so hard that she didn't even notice Freddie and Flossie standing there.

"Hi, Darryl," Freddie said as he got to the door. "What was Jennifer doing here?"

Flossie punched him in the arm. "We were, uh, surprised to see her," she told Darryl.

Darryl shrugged, scratching his curly black hair. "She just came over," he said. "She's been acting a little strange lately. Anyway, what do you guys want?"

"Can we look at your collections again?" Freddie asked. It was the best way he could think of to check out Darryl's room.

Darryl was happy to show them his coins.

"See this one?" he said, pointing to an old, worn-out silver coin with a big eagle on it. "Don't touch it, okay? It's going to be worth over a thousand dollars some day. The one next to it is already worth fifteen bucks."

No matter what coin he showed them, all Darryl seemed interested in was how much money it was worth. He explained how he figured out the value of each coin.

About half an hour later Freddie and Flossie got up to go.

"I'm dizzy from all that money talk," Freddie said as soon as they were out of the house.

"It's sort of creepy. I mean, it's not like he cares about the coins or anything."

Freddie nodded. "Maybe Darryl stole the ball so he could sell it and get the money right away."

"Maybe," Flossie said. "But Darryl seems pretty honest to me. Besides, we don't have any proof. Just a reason why he might have done it."

"True," Freddie agreed. "Still, you never know." He looked at his list. "Marty Peck's next."

"Can't we skip Marty?" Flossie asked. "You know he didn't do it. We know him really well."

"Maybe he saw something important," Freddie said.

"Wouldn't he have told us already if he did?"

"Maybe he didn't realize it was important." Freddie shrugged. "Let's go talk to him, anyway." They ran off toward Marty's house.

Mrs. Peck answered the front door. "Marty's upstairs, cleaning his room," she said. "I told him he couldn't come down until he finished. That boy and his room—honestly!"

Freddie and Flossie ran upstairs and pushed open Marty's door. That was hard to do because so much stuff was piled behind the door.

Marty's room was a complete mess. His stuff was all over the place.

In the middle of the mess sat Marty himself. He was rummaging through mountains of fancy soda cans, sticker books, paper clips, bottle caps, bars of soap from hotels, erasers, and fortunes from fortune cookies. Marty collected *everything*.

"Oh, no!" Marty wailed. "I can't find it anywhere!"

"Find what, Marty?" Freddie asked.

"My hologram sticker," he said. "It's missing!"

Freddie and Flossie immediately joined in the search. They went through everything in Marty's room. There wasn't a paper clip or an eraser they didn't turn over. But Marty was right—the hologram sticker was gone.

"I hate to say it, Marty," Flossie said finally. "But the thief has struck again!"

5

Sneaking Suspicions

Marty sniffed back tears. "I don't get it," he kept saying over and over.

"Marty," Freddie said, "when was the last time you saw your hologram sticker?"

"At the block party," Marty answered. "I took the sticker and my best soda can with me to dinner. I put them on the table while I ate. The sticker was under the can."

"What made that sticker so important to you, Marty?" Flossie asked gently. "I didn't get a chance to see it at the block party."

"It had my favorite dinosaur on it," Marty

said, with a gulp. "Also, if you put it in the sun, it sparkled."

"Gosh," Flossie said, impressed. "It sounds beautiful."

Marty nodded sadly. "I got it as a prize in school for reading twenty books."

"Wait a minute, Marty. Did you ever leave the table you were eating at?" Freddie asked.

"Only when Kevin's baseball was taken. I went over to your table to see what was happening," Marty said.

"Was the sticker still there when you got back to the table?" Flossie asked.

"That's what's driving me nuts," Marty said, suddenly jumping up. "I can't remember whether I went back to the table or not. I was so busy thinking about Kevin's stolen baseball."

"Think, Marty, think," Flossie told him.

Marty scratched his head. "I know I went back to the tent to make sure nobody had touched my gum wrappers."

"Then what did you do?" Freddie asked.

"Then I can't remember what I did!" Marty cried.

"Hold on," Flossie said, excited. "Where's your best soda can?"

"Right over here," Marty said, walking over to a shelf full of empty aluminum cans. He picked out a green and pink can. "It's from Australia."

"You said you put the sticker under the can," Flossie said. "That means you must have gone back to the dinner table to get the can."

"That's right," Marty said, slapping his hand on his knee.

"So the sticker was already missing," Freddie said.

"Which means someone took it at the block party!" Flossie cried. "Just like Kevin's baseball."

"Boy, that's low," Marty said, disgusted.

"Well, don't worry. Because the person who stole your sticker isn't going to get away with it," Freddie promised.

"We'll get your sticker back for you, Marty," Flossie said. "You can count on it."

But when the twins were outside again and on their way home, Flossie didn't seem so sure.

"Do you really think we'll be able to solve this case?" she asked Freddie.

"I sure hope so," Freddie said. "I also hope the thief doesn't strike again. A lot of kids will be upset if more things are taken."

"Poor Marty and Kevin," Flossie said.

Nan and Bert were out on the front steps when Freddie and Flossie got home. "Where have you guys been?" Nan asked. "Mom's been calling all over the neighborhood for you."

"At Marty Peck's," Freddie said. "His hologram sticker is missing."

"And we saw Jennifer Silverstein go into the Lakeport Hobby Shop. We think she might have sold the baseball," Flossie added.

"Whoa, hold on there!" Bert said. "Start from the beginning."

When Freddie and Flossie had told them everything, Bert said, "Good work, you two."

"We sure have a lot of suspects," Nan said with a small grin. "Too many, I think."

"What did you find out today?" Freddie asked, looking from Nan to Bert.

"I followed Danny around all day," Bert said.

"He was acting really suspicious. He kept look-ing over his shoulder to see if anyone was watching him. He had one of those funny looks on his face, like he was up to something sneaky."

"I know the look you mean," said Freddie, gritting his teeth.

"After school he headed toward the pizza place down the block," Bert went on. "At least, that's where I thought he was going. But a bunch of kids got between me and Danny, and I lost him in the crowd. He wasn't at the pizza place. I don't know where he went. What happened with Steve, Nan?"

"Well, I asked Steve about the missing base-ball," Nan told them. "He said he didn't take it, but he might have been lying."

"So what do we do now?" Flossie asked.

"I know what *I'm* going to do," Freddie said. "I'm going to ride my bike over to the gro-cery store so I can play a game of Micro-charger."

"You'd better ask Mom first, Freddie," Nan said. "It's almost dinnertime. And she's already mad at you for not coming straight home after school."

Mrs. Bobbsey made Freddie wait until he had eaten something. "You can go and play *one* game. But be back before dark."

As soon as he'd finished eating, Freddie got on his bike and raced off. When he got to the store, he parked outside and went in.

He was on his way to the back, where the video games were, when he heard two boys talking—Danny Rugg and Steve Frazier!

Freddie quickly ducked behind a wall so they wouldn't see him. They didn't. Steve was just finishing a game of Microcharger. Danny stood next to him, unwrapping a candy bar.

"Tonight I break ten thousand points, no matter what," Steve was saying. "I have five bucks' worth of quarters if I need them."

Wow, thought Freddie. Where did Steve get that kind of money? Kevin had said that Steve was always broke.

"By the way, that nosy Nan Bobbsey was bugging me about my cousin's baseball today," Steve told Danny. "I know she thinks I took it."

"Don't worry about her," Danny said. He took a big bite out of his candy bar. "Mmmphmmm," he added.

"What?" Steve said.

Danny swallowed and said, "Why are you so afraid of Nan Bobbsey?"

"I'm not afraid of her," Steve said. "It's just that—well, I did threaten Kevin, remember?"

"So what?" Danny said.

"And the Bobbseys are detectives, right?" Steve said. "They might get me in trouble."

"You're a dweeb, Frazier," Danny said with a mean laugh. "I can't believe you care what those stupid Bobbseys think. Don't worry about it, okay? I've already taken care of them."

"Huh? What do you mean?" Steve asked.

Danny chuckled. "Never mind," he said. "You'll find out. So will the Bobbseys." He wiped his messy hands on his shirt. "And I can't wait to see the looks on their faces when they do."

6

Buried Treasure

Freddie gulped. What kind of trick did Danny Rugg have in mind? Hoping to hear more, Freddie stayed as still as he could and listened hard. But all Danny talked about was Microcharger. He and Steve played four games.

"You're zapped, Microman," Danny kept saying. "Take this!"

Freddie's legs began to ache. He backed away from the wall. He left the store silently and ran to his bike. It was already starting to get dark. Freddie raced back home.

"Freddie Bobbsey!" his mother said the minute he opened the front door. "Didn't I tell you to come home before dark?"

"Sorry, Mom," Freddie mumbled. "I was going to, but then—"

"Don't give me any buts," his mother said.

Freddie was afraid she was going to ground him. Then how would he ever find Kevin's baseball?

"I don't want this to happen again," she added sternly.

"Okay, Mom," Freddie said. "Sorry."

Mrs. Bobbsey smiled and gave him a quick hug. "Okay, then."

Freddie ran up the stairs to tell his brother and sisters about Steve and Danny.

Bert was doing his homework. Nan was listening to a tape, and Flossie was coloring.

"Come into my room, everybody!" Freddie called out. "I've got big news!"

"Hmm," said Bert after Freddie had filled them in. "Sounds like Steve Frazier didn't steal the ball after all."

"It was Danny, right?" Freddie said.

"We don't know that yet, Freddie," Nan said.

"But he said he's already taken care of us," Flossie piped up.

"True," said Nan. "But we don't know what that means yet. After all, it was Kevin's ball that was stolen, not something of ours. Right now Danny's just one of our suspects."

"Right," Bert agreed. "Let's stay with our plan. Who do you guys still need to talk to?"

Freddie took the folded list out of his pocket. Flossie held it up so they could all see it.

"Elizabeth Chin and Carol Meeker are the only ones left," Freddie said. "What if it's not one of them?"

Bert frowned. "We'll worry about that later, I guess," he said.

The next day after school Freddie and Flossie made sure to stop at home before they went out detecting. They didn't want their mom to be mad at them again.

After a few carrot sticks and crackers, they asked her if they could go over to a friend's house on the block. Mrs. Bobbsey said yes.

They walked over to Elizabeth's house. She showed them her collection of dolls again. Flossie was fascinated, but Freddie felt bored. He'd seen them already, at the block party. He didn't care much about dolls, anyway.

"Elizabeth, try to remember. Did you see anyone near Kevin's table?" he asked her. "After he went to dinner, I mean?"

Elizabeth shook her head. "No," she said. "I went to dinner right after Kevin left. We all did. Of course, we all had to pass by Kevin's display on the way out of the tent. But I didn't see anyone stop there, if that's what you mean."

Elizabeth couldn't tell Freddie and Flossie anything else, so they went to Carol Meeker's house.

"My miniatures aren't worth much money," Carol said. She opened the shoe box where she kept her collection. "But they're really important to me."

Freddie could see why. Looking at the tiny treasures, he felt like a giant in a very small world.

"Carol, did you see anyone by Kevin's table just before you left?" Flossie asked.

"I was the last one out of the tent," Carol said. "So I can tell you for sure. That old baseball was right on the table. I saw it because it was all by itself, right in the middle. Whoever took it must have sneaked back in while we were all eating."

"But that's impossible," Flossie said. "We were sitting right by the entrance. Nobody could have gotten inside without at least *one* of us seeing."

"Well, the ball was there when I left," Carol said again. She started to put her collection away, piece by piece.

"What about Marty Peck's sticker?" Flossie asked. "Did you see that at the block party?"

"Sure, he had it with his soda cans," Carol said. "Is it missing, too?" She looked surprised.

Freddie nodded.

"We think somebody took the sticker from the table where he was eating," Flossie said.

"Marty loses a lot of things, you know," Carol said. "Maybe he just lost it."

"Maybe," Freddie said. But he didn't believe it. "Well, thanks for helping, Carol. Now Flossie and I have to get home."

The twins hurried out of Carol's house and ran down the street to their house. Bert and Nan were waiting for them out front.

"It isn't Elizabeth or Carol," Flossie said firmly. "Carol just likes little things, and Elizabeth collects only dolls. They aren't greedy, either. So I don't see why they would want the ball."

"You're probably right," Nan agreed. "But—"

Just then Chief ran right past them. He had another white ball in his mouth! Bert looked at the others. "Hold everything," he said.

"I know what you're thinking—Chief!" Nan added. "Come on, everyone!"

With that the Bobbseys raced after their speeding puppy. Maybe Chief was the block party thief after all!

Chief ran to a small group of trees in the MacKays' backyard. "Let's see what he does," Nan whispered as they hid behind a bush.

Chief didn't see them. First he dropped the ball. Then he started digging madly.

Soon he had made a hole about eight inches deep. Chief nosed the ball into the hole and covered it with dirt again. Then he ran off, his tongue hanging out happily.

"Let's go!" Bert said, leading the others to the hole. They all dug for a few seconds. At the bottom of the hole they found six baseballs!

Freddie's heart was pounding. Surely one of these balls would be Kevin's.

But none of them had Johnny Kellogg's autograph on them. They were just baseballs that must have been left lying around in kids' yards.

"Chief's starting a collection of his own, I guess," Bert said.

Nobody laughed. They were all too disappointed. Sadly they headed home, wondering what to do next. As they reached the porch, Flossie said, "Hey, look! There's something sticking out of the mailbox."

That was strange, Freddie thought. It was already getting dark. Their mom must have taken in the mail hours ago.

Bert went up to the box and took out something shiny. It was about the size of a baseball card. "Hey, what's this?" he asked, holding it up.

Freddie knew what it was right away. "That's Marty Peck's missing hologram sticker!"

7

Looking for Trouble

"I don't believe it!" Flossie gasped. "The thief gave Marty's sticker back!"

"But why did the thief give it to us?" asked Nan, puzzled. "Look inside the box again, Bert."

This time Bert pulled out an index card. " 'So much for the great detectives,' " he read. The letters were cut out from magazine ads.

"I bet Danny Rugg did this," Freddie said. He took the hologram sticker from Bert. "He said he was going to get us."

"I don't understand, Freddie," said Flossie. "What was he trying to do?"

"Remember, Flossie," Bert said, "Danny doesn't know Freddie overheard him. Maybe he put the sticker in our mailbox to make us look guilty."

"Nobody would ever think we were guilty of stealing," Flossie said.

"Maybe Danny thought it would make us look dumb," Bert said. "You know—if the sticker was right under our noses and we couldn't find it."

"I'm sure Danny did it," Flossie said. "And I bet he took the baseball, too."

Nan frowned. "If he did take the baseball, we need proof, Flossie," she said. "Also, it's one thing to steal a sticker, as a prank. It's another thing to steal a fifty-dollar baseball."

"Oh, well," said Freddie. He put the sticker carefully in his jeans pocket. "At least Marty Peck will be happy. But we sure aren't getting any closer to finding the missing baseball."

Just then Mrs. Bobbsey came out onto the porch. "Suppertime," she announced.

Suddenly Freddie realized he was starving. He

ran inside. The other twins weren't far behind him.

"Hi there, you guys," Mr. Bobbsey called. He was putting a bowl of steaming string beans on the dining room table. "Any luck finding the Johnny Kellogg baseball yet?"

As the twins set the table, they filled their parents in on the case.

"We still don't know who did it," Freddie said, sounding discouraged.

"Well, I haven't had a very good day, either," Mrs. Bobbsey said as they all sat down.

Mr. Bobbsey looked over at his wife. "What's the matter, Mary?" he asked.

"I got a call today," she began, "from the company we rented the tent from."

"The block party tent?" Flossie asked.

"Yes, Flossie. The woman there said they won't give us back our deposit money. They say the tent was damaged."

Bert dropped his fork. "How was it damaged?" he asked excitedly.

"Well," said Mrs. Bobbsey, reaching for the

bread, "they said there was a long slit in the back of the tent. They said it was carefully taped with clear tape. That explains why nobody noticed it when they took the tent down. Now, how in the world—?"

"A slit?" Nan repeated. "You mean someone made a *hole* in the tent?"

"That's it!" Bert said. "We know the ball was in the tent when the last collector left. And we know that no one went in the entrance during dinner."

"So the thief went in through the back," Nan said.

"Through the slit!" added Mrs. Bobbsey, looking shocked and angry. "Well, isn't that something?"

The twins rushed through the rest of their dinner. "We have to get back to the scene of the crime, Mom," Nan explained as they rushed out the door. "It'll be dark soon, and we won't be able to see anything."

In a flash the twins ran down to the MacKays' house and rang the bell. Mr. MacKay came to the door, holding his newspaper.

"Can we look for clues in your yard, Mr. MacKay?" Flossie asked. "It's really important." She gave him her most charming smile.

Mr. MacKay laughed. "Still working on that missing baseball case, huh?" he asked. "Well, sure, why not? Just don't trample Mrs. MacKay's flowers, all right?"

"We won't," Bert promised him. "Thanks, Mr. MacKay."

The twins went to work. "This is where the front entrance of the tent was," Freddie said, pointing to a bare spot on the lawn. "See all the footprints? They're still here."

"That's because it hasn't rained since the party," Bert explained. "Those footprints look as hard as cement."

"Hey," Nan said. "Do you think . . . ?"

"Right!" Bert cried, snapping his fingers. "There might be footprints at the back of the tent!"

The older twins paced out the distance they thought it would be to the back of the tent.

"Hey, Freddie," Bert called as they went

along the side of the MacKays' giant hedge. "This is about where you found that pin, right?"

Freddie nodded. "Yep."

"Maybe the pin came off the thief's jacket while he was squeezing between the tent and the hedge," Flossie said.

"Good thinking, Flossie," Nan told her. Flossie looked pleased.

"But the man in the hobby shop said it was a college pin," Freddie pointed out. "And all of the collectors were kids."

"The thief doesn't have to be one of the collectors," Bert said. "Anybody could have sneaked around to the back of the tent during dinner and made that slit, probably with a knife."

"Footprints!" Nan said suddenly. She was bending down, holding apart two clumps of grass.

Bert ran over to her. He fished out the superpowerful flashlight from his Rex Sleuther crime-solver kit. Then he handed it to Freddie, who shone the light on the footprints.

"I don't get it," Freddie said, looking down at the footprints. "Those are some kid's prints. But a kid wouldn't have a college pin."

The footprints were wide but very small.

"I guess it was a big kid," said Nan. "But whoever it was didn't wear sneakers. The prints are smooth."

Freddie thought for a moment. "Weren't all the kids wearing sneakers that day?" he asked.

"I don't remember," Flossie said.

"Me, neither," Nan admitted.

"It doesn't matter," said Bert. "Let's make a tracing of this footprint."

He took out a sheet of paper and a pencil from his kit. Then he carefully traced the outline of the footprint.

"Nobody had a reason to be back here that day—except the thief." His eyes shone as he looked up at the others.

"I know," said Freddie excitedly. "Tomorrow we can try that tracing on all of our suspects. It'll be just like Cinderella."

Bert nodded. "Somebody out there is guilty."
He held up the picture of the footprint. "And
with this we're going to find out exactly who it
is."

8

If the Shoe Fits . . .

All of the twins were excited the next morning as they set off for school. Each of them was carrying a tracing of the footprint.

"How are we going to get kids to put their feet on the tracing?" Flossie asked.

"I'm sure you'll figure out a way," Nan said, laughing. "Use some charm."

Flossie grinned. "Okay. But what is Freddie going to use?" she joked.

"Hey!" Freddie said, frowning. But when he saw the others laughing, he mumbled, "Oh, never mind."

Suddenly Nan poked Freddie in the ribs with

her elbow. "Carol Meeker is coming out of her house," she said. "Want to see if her footprint matches the drawing?"

"Carol didn't take Kevin's baseball," Flossie said.

"She didn't? How do you know?" Bert asked.

"I just know," Flossie insisted.

"Well, until we find out who did take the ball, everyone is a suspect," Nan said. Then she called out, "Hi, Carol! Want to walk with us?"

Carol waved and ran up to the Bobbseys. "Sure," she said.

They all turned onto Elm Street and headed for Lakeport Elementary School. "Wait, guys," Nan said, stopping. "My shoelace is untied."

Freddie noticed that Nan's shoelace was perfectly fine. But the way she bent down to fix it was very convincing.

Carol stopped walking to wait for Nan. Her foot was right under Nan's nose. "Oops!" cried Nan as her notebook tumbled from her arm.

Freddie grinned. Nan was being clumsy on purpose.

Nan fumbled to pick up the notebook. It fell

open to the page with the tracing. Freddie saw that Nan had bent the page back so it would do just that. Nan's eyes darted from Carol's foot to the tracing.

"Here," said Carol. "I'll help you." She bent down to pick up the notebook.

"It's okay, I've got it," said Nan, straightening up. "Let's go."

When everyone was walking again, Nan signaled the others behind Carol's back. "It's not her," she mouthed, shaking her head.

"I'm going to run ahead," Carol said when they got near the school. "I see my friend. Bye!"

"One down," Bert said. "If we count only kids who were at the block party, we've got about twenty to go."

"Hey! Look who I see," Flossie whispered when they reached the entrance of the school. There stood Jennifer Silverstein, talking to another girl.

"I'm going to find out if she's the Cinderella we're looking for," Flossie said. "You stay here."

Her brothers and sister stayed behind as Flossie ran up to Jennifer. "Hi, Jennifer,"

Flossie said, smiling. "Oh, I love your shoes! Are they new?"

Jennifer looked confused. She stuck out one foot. "They used to be new," she said. "A few months ago."

It was easy to see that Jennifer couldn't be the culprit. Even though she was tall, her foot was slender, not stubby like the footprint.

"So much for her," Flossie told her brothers and sister after Jennifer turned and walked into the school.

Just then the warning bell rang. "I want to check out Elizabeth Chin before the late bell rings," Flossie said, hurrying inside. "Bye, Nan! Bye, Bert! See you later, Freddie." She hurried inside.

Bert and Nan had to continue on to Lakeport Middle School. Freddie stood with them for a minute.

"Elizabeth is tiny. That footprint must be Steve's or Danny's," Freddie insisted. "They're the only kids with feet big enough to fit the prints."

"There they are now. Steve walks his little

sister to school, too," Nan said. "They're over by the water fountain."

"How are we ever going to get their prints? They'd never fall for your trick the way Carol did," Freddie said.

"Don't worry," Bert said. "I have an idea." He walked over to the water fountain and leaned over it. "Hi, Danny," he said, in a friendly way. "Hi, Steve."

Danny and Steve shot Bert weird looks. "Hey, Bobbsey," Danny mumbled.

Bert took a sip of water. Suddenly he put his finger over the waterspout. That sent water splashing all over the place.

"Hey! Watch out, Bobbsey!" Danny complained. "You're getting me all wet, you loser!"

"Sorry, guys," Bert said, bending down to drink again. "My finger must have slipped."

"Jerk," Danny said under his breath. "Come on, Steve. Let's get out of here before we get another shower."

The two boys walked away, glaring at Bert. Freddie and Nan walked up to Bert. "What was *that* all about?" Nan asked.

Bert grinned. "Look!" He pointed to the ground. The boys' wet shoes had made footprints!

"Not bad, Bert," Nan said, laughing. She knelt down and compared the footprints to her tracing. "They're close," she said with a sigh, "but not quite big enough."

"Gee," Freddie said. "Danny and Steve have really big feet!"

"You're right about that," said Bert. "I've heard kids calling Steve 'Bigfoot.' Danny's feet are even bigger."

"Do you think the footprints could have been made by a grown-up?" Freddie asked.

Nan looked confused. "It would explain the college pin," she admitted. "But why would a grown-up steal Kevin's ball? It was worth only fifty dollars, right? That's a lot for a kid, but it's not that much to a grown-up. Unless, of course, the thief is a big Johnny Kellogg fan."

The twins split up and headed off to school. It was a frustrating day for Freddie. He tried his tracing against the feet of every kid he saw from his block, but none of them fit.

He was sitting in class, waiting for the dismissal bell to ring, when an idea suddenly hit him. Nan was right about one thing—fifty dollars wasn't a lot of money to a grown-up. Not enough to be worth stealing.

But how did the twins know the ball was worth only fifty dollars? Mr. Sher had offered Kevin fifty, but what if the ball was worth more?

As soon as the bell rang, Freddie went over to Flossie. "Tell Mom I'll be home soon," he said. "I have to check something out."

"Can't I go, too?" asked his twin.

"I'm already in trouble with Mom," Freddie said. "I need you to cover for me."

Flossie crossed her arms.

"I'll give you half my bubble gum," he said, taking out a piece of gum and ripping it in half.

"Deal," said Flossie with a grin. She popped the gum in her mouth and left.

Freddie headed quickly down the street, straight for the Lakeport Hobby Shop.

Once inside, he walked up to the man behind the counter. "Excuse me," Freddie said. "I'm interested in buying an autographed baseball. Do you have any?"

"Oh, it's you again," said the man, looking at Freddie over the top of his glasses. "Why, yes, we have some. How much did you want to spend?"

"About fifty dollars," said Freddie.

The man brought out a tray full of balls. Most of the signatures were hard to read.

"Do you have any Johnny Kellogg baseballs?" Freddie asked. "I'd be really interested in one of them."

"I've never seen a Johnny Kellogg ball," the man said. "They're rare—and very expensive."

"Really?" Freddie said. "Like, how expensive? More than fifty dollars?"

The man laughed, as if Freddie had just told a funny joke. "Fifty dollars?" he repeated. "Son, if you can find one for fifty dollars, grab it. Why, a Johnny Kellogg baseball is worth at least a thousand dollars."

Freddie's jaw dropped. "What?" he said.

"You heard me," the man said. "One thousand dollars!"

9

Caught!

Freddie raced home as fast as he could. Kevin's baseball was worth a thousand dollars! In his wildest dreams Freddie had never imagined a baseball could be worth that much.

At the corner he ran into Mr. Anderson and Mr. Sher. Mr. Anderson was loading a suitcase into the back of his station wagon. "Hi there, Freddie," he called. "How's it going?"

"Great, Mr. Anderson!" Freddie said. "We're hot on the trail of Kevin's missing baseball."

Mr. Sher raised his eyebrows. "Well, what do you know?" he said. "Ace detectives, eh? Good

73

for you. Sorry I won't be around when you catch the thief."

"Shorty's leaving a few days early," Mr. Anderson explained. "I'm taking him to the train station right now."

"It was nice meeting all you kids," said Mr. Sher.

Freddie waved goodbye and ran home. Quickly he told his brother and sisters what he'd learned at the hobby shop.

"That's amazing!" said Bert. He whistled. "A thousand dollars! I'll bet the thief was a grown-up after all."

Nan sighed. "Bert, there must have been fifty grown-ups at the block party. How are we ever going to try the footprint on all of them?"

Bert frowned. "It *would* take a long time," he admitted.

"I give up," Flossie said. "That footprint was too wide for a kid and too small for most grown-ups. So who does it belong to?"

"Hey!" Bert snapped his fingers. "What about that guy Mr. Sher? He's the one who offered to buy the ball for fifty dollars!"

"He's really short, too," Nan added. "And kind of chubby. He might have wide feet."

"I'll bet you a Johnny Kellogg baseball you're right," Bert said, grinning. "I think we might have solved our mystery."

Freddie bit his lip. "Uh-oh. I have bad news, guys."

"What is it, Freddie?" Flossie asked.

"Mr. Sher just left for the train station. We're too late."

Bert jumped up. "Maybe not," he said. "The station's only about twenty minutes away by bike."

Nan shook her head. "He'll probably be long gone by then."

"It's our only chance," Bert said. "Come on, gang. Let's put on some speed."

The twins were on their bikes in no time. But as they started for the corner, they saw Mr. Anderson pulling his station wagon back into his driveway.

"Mr. Anderson!" Nan called out. "Is Mr. Sher already on his train?"

Mr. Anderson checked his watch. "Hmm,"

he said. "I don't think so. His train's not due for another five minutes."

"Five minutes!" Flossie groaned.

"We'll never make it there on our bikes," Freddie said.

"What's the matter, kids?" Mr. Anderson asked.

"Can you give us a ride to the station, Mr. Anderson?" Bert asked. "It's super important."

"Well, sure," Mr. Anderson said, looking puzzled. "But why?"

"We'll tell you on the way," Nan said. "We have to get to Mr. Sher before he boards that train!"

The twins were all piling into the wagon when Chief ran by. The puppy had another white ball in his mouth. There were two little kids running after him, yelling for Chief to give it back.

Chief jumped right into the wagon with the Bobbseys. Bert took the ball out of the puppy's mouth and threw it back to the little kids.

"Can Chief come with us?" Nan asked Mr.

Anderson. "He's off his leash again, and we don't want him getting into any more trouble."

Mr. Anderson laughed. "Oh, all right," he said, pulling the wagon out of the driveway. "My dog rides with me all the time. So what's this whole thing about, anyway?"

"We're sorry to have to say this," Nan told him. "But we think your friend Mr. Sher may be a thief."

Freddie thought Mr. Anderson would be upset. Instead their neighbor just sighed. "Nothing about Shorty would surprise me," he said. "He's a man who never really grew up."

"But he's your friend," Flossie pointed out.

Mr. Anderson shook his head. "Well, Flossie, I don't know if I'd really call him a friend. He and I went to college together, but that was a long time ago. Before this last visit I hadn't seen Shorty in over ten years."

"Wow," said Flossie.

"College," Nan murmured. "That pin we found—"

"Shorty did lose his college fraternity pin,"

Mr. Anderson said. "He was looking all over for it the night of the block party."

"We've just got to get to the station in time!" Freddie said, leaning forward in his seat.

It took them six minutes to reach the station. The twins had told Mr. Anderson the whole story by then. "I sure hope we're not too late," he said.

As the Bobbseys got out of the wagon, they heard a long train whistle. "Come on!" Bert shouted. "Run!"

In no time they reached the platform. Mr. Sher was still there. He was holding his suitcase, waiting for the train doors to open.

"What—?" Mr. Sher said as Bert ran up to him. "Excuse me, but I'm in a hurry."

"Not so fast," said Bert, standing between Mr. Sher and the train door. Nan bent down and compared the tracing to Mr. Sher's shoes.

"It fits exactly!" she cried. Then she frowned. "Mr. Sher, you should be ashamed of yourself."

Mr. Sher seemed frozen to the spot. "What?" he said. "I don't know what you're talking about. I have a train to catch."

"All aboard!" shouted the conductor. The train doors opened.

"Get out of my way, kid," Mr. Sher said rudely, pushing Bert aside. Mr. Sher put one foot up onto the train step.

Suddenly Chief burst onto the platform. Seeing Bert in danger, he growled and leapt at Mr. Sher. The big puppy landed right on the little man's arm. The suitcase went tumbling to the ground with a crash, and the lid popped open. Then something white and round rolled out onto the platform.

There, for everyone to see, was Kevin Frazier's Johnny Kellogg baseball. Before anybody could say anything, Chief gave a loud bark. He jumped at the ball, took it in his mouth, and raced back down the platform!

10

The Game Is Up

"Hey! Stop that dog!" shouted Mr. Sher.

Mr. Anderson came up and grabbed him by the arm. "Shorty, I'm ashamed of you," he said. "Don't you remember our old college pledge? 'Honest to the end'?"

Mr. Sher looked at the ground. "I *am* ashamed, I guess," he mumbled. "I never did learn to work for my money. All these years I've let my relatives support me. Then, every so often, I'd go visit my old college friends. Most of them have done pretty well for themselves. Wherever I go, I—I, uh, take a little something valuable with me when I leave."

"Well, those days are over now," said Mr. Anderson sternly. He looked at the twins. "And you can thank the Bobbseys here for putting a stop to it all."

Mr. Sher shook his head sadly. "I guess Kevin felt pretty bad about losing his ball," he said.

"You bet he did," Bert said angrily.

"His grandfather gave him that baseball, you mean man," Flossie scolded.

"Well, when you give the ball back to him, I hope you'll apologize for me." Suddenly Mr. Sher pulled away from Mr. Anderson and started running for the train. At any minute it would pull out of the station. Mr. Anderson raced after him and stopped him.

"You can apologize to Kevin yourself, Shorty," he said angrily. "You're not going anywhere. Not yet. Not until you tell the whole story to the Lakeport police."

"Oh, by the way," Flossie said, fishing the college pin out of her pocket. "I think this will count as evidence, Mr. Anderson."

Mr. Anderson took the pin and looked at it.

The train whistle tooted as the train pulled out of the station.

With a defeated look, Mr. Sher watched it go. "Oh, well," he said. "I guess I couldn't go on like this forever." Hanging his head, he followed them back to Mr. Anderson's car.

"What about Chief?" Mr. Anderson asked the Bobbseys. "Don't you want to go after him?"

"That's okay, Mr. Anderson," Nan said. "He knows a secret way home, through the woods. He's got a special place where he buries things, too."

Mr. Sher gave a sad little laugh. "That dog is a better thief than I am," he said.

An hour later Freddie, Flossie, Bert, and Nan stood around Chief's secret hiding place. Nan held Chief by the leash.

Kevin Frazier and Marty Peck stood with them. Marty was smiling. He had his hologram sticker in his hand.

"You know," Nan said, "I felt sorry for Mr. Sher in a way."

"He looked pretty unhappy when the police came," Bert said.

"Sure he was unhappy. That's 'cause he got caught!" Marty said.

The other kids laughed.

"Well, are we going to dig up the ball or not?" Flossie asked.

"Here goes," Bert said. He pushed a shovel into the soft ground.

"Careful, Bert," Kevin warned.

"No problem," Bert said. As soon as he loosened the earth, he knelt down and started digging with his fingers.

"Here it is, Kevin," he said at last. In his hand was the Johnny Kellogg baseball.

"It doesn't look damaged at all," Kevin said happily as he took the ball from Bert. "Just a little wet. I was afraid Chief might have left tooth marks on it."

"No way," said Flossie. "Chief may be big, but he's the gentlest dog in the world. He wouldn't hurt anything or anybody—not even a crook like Mr. Sher."

"There they are!" Freddie heard someone say.

He turned around and saw his mother coming toward him. Jennifer Silverstein was with her.

"Congratulations on finding Kevin's baseball," Jennifer said.

Kevin had a wide smile. "Thank goodness for the Bobbseys!" he said.

Bert told his mother exactly how they had nabbed Mr. Sher. "I'm impressed," she said, "but not surprised. You kids are terrific."

Soon everyone started walking home. Jennifer turned to Nan and grinned. "I'll bet you all thought I took that baseball," she said.

Nan blushed. "Well," she said, "when you're trying to solve a case, you have a lot of suspects."

"I know you guys asked about me at the collector's shop," Jennifer said with a giggle. "The man who owns it is my uncle."

"We didn't know that," Nan admitted.

"Well, what were you talking to him about?" Flossie asked impatiently. "You sure looked like you had a secret."

Jennifer reached in her knapsack and took out a beautiful copper coin. "It's for Darryl," she said shyly. "His birthday is tomorrow."

"Oh, I get it," Nan said.

"You have a crush on Darryl Williams?" Flossie asked Jennifer loudly.

"Flossie!" Nan said.

"I guess so," Jennifer said, looking embarrassed.

"See?" Flossie said.

"Oh, and there's something else," Jennifer added, reaching into her pack again. This time she pulled out a pink leather autograph book. "I want your autographs—all of you."

"*Our* autographs?" Freddie asked, looking confused.

"Sure," Jennifer said. "I think your signatures are going to be worth a lot of money someday. After all, it's not everyone who'll have the autographs of the world's greatest detectives!"